DEEPEST DARKNESS

Deepest Darkness

DENISE HAYWARD

DERNIER PUBLISHING
Tonbridge

First published 2010

Published by Dernier Publishing
P.O. Box 403, Tonbridge, TN9 9BJ, England
www.dernierpublishing.com

ISBN 978 0 9536963 6 9

Book design and production for the publisher by
Bookprint Creative Services, <www.bookprint.co.uk>
Printed in Great Britain.

To Fred
Companion and encourager
"treasures in the darkness"

one

I awoke, terrified, sweat pouring off me. I was screaming, screaming, screaming. I don't remember if I was screaming words or simply screaming. I have no memory of the dream. I never did. It happened frequently. A nightmare would creep into my sleep but I would remember nothing except the utter sense of terror.

Mum came to me in her dressing gown. She sat me on her lap and wrapped her arms around me. She would rock me and sing to me. She didn't sing words she just hummed beautiful tunes that she made up. It was so beautiful it always made me think of angels. Gradually my heart quietened and I felt peaceful and safe in Mum's arms.

When I was a child of ten I came to this island full of fear. Fearful of being alone – never having known true solitude, fearful of the dark – never having known darkness without any man-made light; fearful of something out there that was going to get me – yet never having faced the wildness that is nature.

We came to this island the first time for a holiday. My mum and dad were tired and needed to get away. Mum was exhausted from constantly disturbed sleep caused by my nightmares. I had been having nightmares since I was a young child. I could never remember a time when I had not had them. But over recent months they had been increasing in frequency. Every night my parents were woken by my screaming. Sometimes two or three times a night. Every time my mum lovingly took me in her arms and sang to me. She always stayed until I was soundly asleep. Sometimes she fell asleep there with me.

No one could understand why I had these nightmares or why I was so fearful. My parents had taken me to the family doctor who had referred me to a child psychiatrist. But no one could find a reason.

I remember one night Daddy came into the room. Mum still held me in her arms singing softly. I was beginning to drift off into peaceful sleep. But I wasn't asleep. My parents thought I was and they spoke in whispers.

"Chris, Chris, Chris," Dad sighed my mum's name and sat on the end of my bed. "What is to be done with our little girl? I can't stand it. I can't stand the disturbed sleep. I can't stand the exhaustion on your face. I can't stand the pain in my little girl." And he wept. I could feel my mum's tears, also, dropping on to my face. I didn't cry myself, although I wanted to. My parents would have been embarrassed to find I was awake.

After a while Daddy stood up and came over to us. He began to stroke my hair softly. "Why don't we go away for a break?" he asked.

"There's no point," she said. "You know how holidays only add to Abi's fear and stress. And to be honest," she held her hand out to my dad, "it only adds to mine."

"Someone at work was telling me about a place in Canada, on Vancouver Island, that is utterly beautiful," he continued, ignoring my mother's objections. "He's been feeling under a lot of pressure and he said he's come home really refreshed. He said there was a peace about the place. 'Almost like paradise' he described it. Christine, maybe it's a place where we could be refreshed. You and me. Ben could run around to his heart's content. Maybe even Abi might find some peace there too."

Mum sighed and yawned. "Abi would never go in an aeroplane. And I can't see that it would do her any good."

"I can't stand it. I want to do something. To do something different. It can't make anything worse for Abi – it might help. We've tried doctors and pills and counselling. None of it's worked. Let's give this a go." Daddy was pleading.

"I can't think about it now. Let's talk about it another time." Mum gently laid me back in bed, kissed my forehead and they left.

I lay thinking, gazing at my night light. I understood how difficult my nightmares and my fears were for my parents. I thought about the place Daddy had described. It did sound lovely. But it would mean a journey and unknown places and I was scared.

I don't know how Daddy persuaded Mum. But clearly they talked about it. A few days later when Mum picked me up from school she had obviously decided to tackle me as we were driving home.

"Did you have a good day, Abi?"

"OK."

"Abi, would you like to go on holiday?"

I panicked inside and didn't answer.

"Would you?" my mum tried again.

"Where?" I managed to ask quietly, remembering I wasn't supposed to know.

"There's a place in Canada your dad would like to go to."

My heart was beating hard. I was expecting it. I had been thinking about it all day and every day since the night I heard Daddy talking about it. I couldn't concentrate on anything else. I lay awake much of the night looking at it from every possible angle. I lived the journey, the holiday in every detail I could imagine. My nightmares intensified. I did not want to go, I could not go. I wanted to cry and stamp my feet. I wanted everything to stay just the way it was. Looking back, it wasn't much of a life, but I could manage it. It was like living in a square with thick black lines marking it out. This holiday would mean stepping out of my clearly marked square. "Where is Canada?" I asked. I knew, I had looked it up in the atlas we have in the lounge. But it meant not having to give an answer yet.

"It's across the Atlantic Ocean, it's north of the United States of America," Mum replied. She was trying to sound light-hearted. I could tell it was really important to her. I felt everything was pressing down hard on me.

"Will we have to fly?" I asked. I knew we'd have to fly. But it delayed the moment I would have to answer. It felt like there were voices in my head screaming "no". But somewhere deeper than my fear I knew my parents really needed this. I couldn't bear to be the reason they couldn't go. And though everything in me did not want to go, somehow, something stronger than my own selfishness and my own fear compelled me to say "yes".

"OK," I said very quietly.

"Oh, darling," my mum said with tears in her eyes. Mum was amazed it could be that easy to get me to agree. But, unknown to her, I had been battling this for days. "I know how hard it is," Mum continued through her surprise. "But we will take care of you all the way and maybe you'll love it."

I wasn't very hopeful.

two

So the holiday was planned. Mum and Dad were excitedly making preparations – booking flights and somewhere to stay. The details went over my head. I didn't want to know about any part of the preparations; I didn't want to go. I didn't want to think about going. I preferred to ignore it and hope it might never happen.

As the days went by it became obvious that this was going to be a major holiday for my parents. We rarely had much in the way of holidays and they were throwing everything into it. We would go during the school summer holidays so that Ben, my six-year-old brother, and I wouldn't have to take any time off school.

Dad decided to take some unpaid leave as well as most of his annual leave from work, so that we could have six weeks away. He was the manager of a garden centre in town. He loved his job. He had started as an assistant when he left school and learned everything he could about plants. He loved gardening and plants and being outside whatever the weather. Occasionally he would take himself off to the countryside somewhere and walk. Usually he would go off for the day but every now and then he'd take a backpack and camp overnight. When he had the chance he loved to go to the Lake District.

Ben and I were amazed how much time they spent looking at books and maps of Canada. They laughed a lot. They tried to involve Ben and me in the plans but I didn't want to know. Ben took an interest for brief moments but he couldn't understand that we weren't going tomorrow. The months seemed like years to him, so he couldn't stay excited.

"Is Canada across the sea?" Ben asked when they first told him we were going.

"Yes," Mum replied.

He thought for a moment. "Does that mean we'll go in a boat?" he asked, his eyes lighting up.

"No," said Dad. "It would take three weeks to get there by boat."

"I'd like to spend three weeks on a boat," he said.

"We'll fly," Dad said.

"Fly!" Ben said with great enthusiasm. He stuck his arms out and ran around the room "flying". Mum and Dad looked at each other and laughed. "Like Dumbo?" he asked. "Or Superman?" He put both arms out in front of him swaying his whole body like he was flying through the air, humming the Superman theme.

"I don't think the outfit would suit me," Dad said.

"Not with your belly," Mum chipped in.

"Dad's not fat," I protested.

"Thanks, Abi," he said. "Still, I think my Superhero days are past. Tell you what, Tigger." Dad always called Ben "Tigger", due to the fact that he bounced everywhere and was as fearless as a tiger. "You can fly like Superman, the rest of us will fly in a plane. How about you, Abi?"

"What?" I said looking up from my book, pretending I wasn't listening.

"How are you going to get to Canada?" Daddy asked. "Are you going to fly in a plane with me and Mum or are you going to hitch a ride with Superman here?"

"If I have to go, couldn't I just beam up?" I said, trying to be light-hearted but thinking how much easier it would be if I could travel that way.

I was sitting on the floor cross-legged, Ben launched himself at me in delight, landing in my lap. "Yeah," he said. "I want to do that, too."

He thought, then he looked at me and gave me a big hug, suddenly getting serious. "I'll go how Abi goes. She needs me to look after her, 'cos I'm braver than her."

I smiled and hugged him back. He could be so sweet sometimes.

"What about Mum and me? We might need you to look after us in the plane," Dad said.

"You'll have to do without me," he said. "I'll show you how to fight the baddies." He dragged Dad down on the floor for a wrestling fight, all thoughts of flying and Canada forgotten for the moment.

The books, leaflets and maps were left on the coffee table in the lounge; I think they were supposed to spark my interest. I completely ignored them – at least I made out that I did. When no one was around, I'd sneak a look at the maps and brochures. I was always fascinated by maps; that the lines, squiggles, names and colours could somehow represent towns and places and countries. But

I was overwhelmed at how far it looked, even on the page of an atlas. All across that huge ocean and all the way across Canada. You could fit loads of Britains into the vast mass on the map that was Canada. And we had to go all the way to the far side of it.

The flight would take about eleven hours. I could hardly imagine being in a plane for eleven hours. In snatched moments studying the brochures, I gathered we would be staying in a log cabin on the beach. I had to admit to myself that the brochure made it look beautiful. It looked like the cabins were right on the beach. There seemed to be several of them together. Although they were on the beach they seemed to be surrounded by a kind of woodland. The beach looked big, so the sea appeared to be far enough away to be safe. I loved the look of the sea but I didn't like to be too close. The pictures showed clear, sparkly water and long, deep sandy beaches with rocky places. Behind the cabins the trees seemed to become a thick massive woodland and then there were mountains.

As I looked, it drew me in. Part of me wanted to go, to see a place so beautiful and different. But it wasn't familiar and I wasn't sure if it was safe, yet there was something peaceful about it. However, there was a long journey to get there. What a pity, I frequently thought, that we couldn't just beam up. As the time got closer, my parents became more and more excited, whilst I became more anxious.

Somehow we arrived there, all of us, in one piece. To this day I don't really remember the flight. Just a sense that it was a great relief for everyone when we arrived –

my parents, the crew, the other passengers and me. I think I screamed a lot.

Even as I try, all these years later, to remember something of the journey, of the flight, I still only recall a sense of panic, no details. I have vague memories of the drive from the airport to our destination on Vancouver Island. It was a long car journey, but I think exhaustion from the flight actually dulled the fear of anything else. My brother Ben and I were carried to bed in our log cabin, sound asleep. Where I, apparently, slept solidly for longer than I ever have. So of our arrival late in the evening, I remember nothing.

"You do in Canada," he said. "That's how they do it here."

"Gross," I repeated. "I'm not having any."

"Well I am," said Dad, pouring it over his bacon.

"I am," Ben shouted. "I'm having lots of it."

"You don't need lots of it, Ben; just a little bit," Mum cautioned.

"I love syrup with bacon," he said.

"You've never had it before," I said.

"I still love it," he replied, picking up the bottle of maple syrup. He turned it upside down over his bacon and shook it.

"Careful," Mum said too late, as it poured over his plate. She grabbed the bottle. We all sat there and laughed. At first Ben looked a bit shocked but as he gazed at his plate overflowing with sweet, sticky syrup, a cheeky grin spread over his cute little face. With his finger and thumb he picked up a slice of bacon, dripping with syrup. He tipped his head back, opened his mouth and let the syrup drip in. Then he sucked the rest of the syrup off and finally ate the bacon.

"This is really nice, Abi. It's the best breakfast I've ever had." And he did exactly the same with the other slice of bacon.

"Why do they have maple syrup on bacon over here, Daddy?" I asked.

"Well, firstly, because it's delicious," he said tucking into his own breakfast. "Secondly, because they've got loads of it over here."

"Why?" asked Ben, wiping his fingers on his T-shirt.

"Because it comes from maple syrup trees, and they have loads of those."

"It doesn't!" said Ben laughing loudly.

"Seriously, Dad," I said. "Why have they got loads of maple syrup?"

He looked at me, pretending to feel hurt. "Why does no one ever believe me? Seriously, it's the sap of the sugar maple tree. They make holes in the bark and collect it. And there it is. Delicious on bacon, Abi." I pulled a face. Neither Ben or I were quite sure whether to believe him about sugar maple trees. I ate my breakfast without it.

four

It was glorious weather and we lived in shorts and T-shirts. We spent each day on the beach. Ben and I would make sandcastles and play games until Ben got bored. He was really drawn by the sea. He was everything I was not – in a word, fearless. The sea held no fear for him at all. He couldn't swim but he loved splashing around in the sea with Daddy. Mummy and I would sit further up the beach reading and chatting and watching. Sometimes we walked, just the two of us. I knew, at times, she longed to be splashing around in the sea with Daddy and Ben. But I just pretended not to notice, I couldn't do anything about it. I couldn't go into the sea and I wouldn't be left by myself. But we had a peaceful time, she was content. She was sleeping better at night because I was sleeping better, most nights.

There was so much to look at on the beach. There were boats out on the sea, speed boats, sailing boats, large passenger boats. I thought how it must be fun to go out in a boat, but I couldn't do that. There were lots of islands, some quite small but some looked big. They were all covered in trees. I imagined people living on them, but I don't think they do. There were usually a few other people on the beach but it wasn't crowded. There was so much space to sit or walk or play.

I loved looking at the black rocks set against the pale grey sand. And always there was the dark green of the forest behind us and in the distance, mountains; not so close as to feel threatening but not far away. It was very like the pictures in the brochures, but seeing it in real life was so much more beautiful, peaceful, and awesome too.

One time all four of us built a very complicated sandcastle with lots of little sandcastles making the turrets and different parts of the castle; it even had a moat. Daddy was the designer and the rest of us his slaves. He said that's what it would have been like when they built the big old castles and cathedrals in Britain a thousand years ago. He was very serious about it, in a fun kind of way.

Sometimes we would all clamber together on the rocks and look into the rock pools. I remember the first starfish we saw. I had never seen anything like it. It was bright orange. There were so many starfish and they were all kinds of colours. The pools were filled with life – little fish and crabs and the most amazing coloured seaweed.

Occasionally Daddy went off by himself walking so Mum was split between me and Ben. Ben always wanted to do something exciting – which usually involved getting wet in the sea. And me, I always kept a certain distance from the sea and anything exciting, which for me, meant frightening.

In the evenings when Ben was in bed, Mum, Daddy and I would sit on the balcony watching the sea and the few people still out on the beach, and the sun slowly setting. Daddy would sit me on his lap and tell me about the things he saw on his walks. The tall trees and the beautiful flowers, the animals and the birds. He had a book about the wildlife of Western Canada. We would look at the pictures and Daddy would tell me about the animals. He told me how he would love to see a bear but, he hoped, from a safe distance. I loved to hear him talk as long as he assured me that no bears were going to come near the cabin or the beach. Those were my places of safety. As long as those places were safe I didn't mind too much if there was danger out in the nearby forests and mountains. It was a peaceful time. It was like we had all relaxed and started to breathe again.

We had been here about two weeks and really got into a routine of what we did each day. I was always happy with a routine, it made me feel safe.

I guess Daddy has never been much of a routine person. Maybe it was all getting a bit too tame for him. There was danger and excitement to be had on our doorstep. He often said that there is no real wilderness in Britain. And here it was all around him and he was only able to touch the edge.

One morning we were enjoying breakfast on the balcony when Daddy made his announcement. "I've been talking to some of the locals and some of the hikers that have been staying here," he said. Mum glanced up at him.

"And?" she said.

"They say that to really experience wilderness you have to spend a night camping out there. With no one else around."

"Really," Mum replied with a slight edge to her voice.

"So I think I will." Silence. The tension evaporated as my mother chuckled. "What's so funny?" he asked in mock offence.

"Well, I was just imagining you meeting a bear without a clue what to do. You can't learn survival skills from a book, you know. These people you've been talking to, they know what they're doing. Most of them have grown up here. It's not the Surrey hills or even the Lake District, you know."

"That, Christine, is the point. It isn't the Surrey hills or the Lake District. That's exactly it. That's what I want. I've talked to these people. I know what to do, now I want to experience it."

"So you're going to camp out in the wilderness for a night?"

"Three nights, actually." Mum gave Daddy an exasperated look.

"So you're going to camp out in the wilderness for three nights, having never seen anything more wild than a fox in your life before? Knowing only what you've read in books about how to survive in the wilderness, not to mention that you're leaving me to look after and entertain the kids by myself for three or four days?"

Dad looked up at her sheepishly, smiling. "Yep."

"And I'm supposed to say fine, no probs. Go and have a wonderful time?"

"That's about it."

She sighed. "And if you get killed by a bear or a rattle snake or something I'm just supposed to say 'Ah well, never mind, he had a nice wilderness experience, let's go home then kids.'"

"Well," he replied. "You could shed a few tears as well. You could even send a search party out."

"Oh forget it. Let's be sensible."

"I'm going. I'm sorry. I'll be fine. I may never have this opportunity again."

"And blow me then. Blow what I would like to do. I'm just the good little wife looking after the kids." She was getting cross. Ben and I looked at each other. Ben rolled his eyes and I tried not to laugh, he always looked so comical when he did it.

"No. We're here for another four weeks. If there's something you want to do you can do it too and I'll look after the kids."

"Oh yeah," Mum retorted. "And when Abi wakes up with a nightmare you'll sing to her. I don't think so! You'd make her nightmares worse." It was a family joke, Dad's singing. His voice was terrible. Ben, always ready to perform, began humming really out of tune, just like Daddy. Mum was being serious but we all burst out laughing. And her anger vanished. "Oh go and do what you need to do then. I thought we were just a normal family. Ha, ha! I have a daughter who is frightened of everything, a son who is frightened of nothing and a husband determined to explore a wilderness he knows nothing about!"

five

It was settled. Daddy was going off into the wilderness, alone. He spent the next few days preparing, getting his gear together, reading all he could on survival in the wilderness. That Friday Daddy set off with his tent and a backpack, which contained food and maps and all that he would need to survive in the wilderness for four days. He also had plenty of conflicting information from the people he had talked to about what to do if he came across a bear. Play dead; don't play dead. Look it in the eye; don't look it in the eye. Well it all depends on what kind of bear it is.

Strangely, for all my fearfulness, I was not fearful of what might happen to my dad. Somehow I believed my dad to be invincible. He'd be fine. He may not know exactly what to do if a bear showed up, but somehow he'd handle it if he had to. Me, I knew I'd never cope, but Dad, he'd be fine. I didn't share Mum's concerns for his safety.

He left early in the morning. It was strange to wave him off. He looked a bit lonely as he walked away. Mum was tense. She was laughing and joking but I could feel it by the way she was holding my hand. I could see it in her smile. I don't think she resented his going but I think she felt he wasn't very well prepared to face the wilderness alone.

It felt very quiet once Daddy left. We all felt a bit empty for a while, but Ben was soon tearing around wanting to do something exciting. "Can we go to the beach?" he asked Mum. Mum sighed.

"I want to have a cup of tea and sit quietly here for a while. Is that all right?"

"It's boring," he replied pouting. "I want to play. Can't Abi take me out?"

Mum glanced at me questioningly. I shook my head frantically and looked down.

"Oh, Abi," he whined. "Won't you? Please," he said drawing it out appealingly, looking his sweetest.

"No," I replied crossly. "You know I don't like going out without Mum or Dad."

"Oh Abi," he whined again. Then he smiled at me. "I'll look after you," he said and meant it.

I smiled but shook my head. "No, I can't Ben," I said firmly.

He held my hand. "You'll be all right. I've been out there playing with my friends, nothing will hurt you. Anyway," he said leaping into a karate pose, "I won't let anything hurt you."

We all laughed. He tried to pull me out of my chair but gave up when I wouldn't budge. He picked up his cricket bat, held it like a gun and started shooting baddies all round the room.

Mum soon realised she wasn't going to get any peace and quiet so she shook off her anxieties and took us to the beach. Ben was soon playing with the friends he had made since we got here. Mum and I walked along the beach barefoot, enjoying the sun on our faces and the sand between our toes.

Later we sat on the beach. Mum was reading. I had a book in my hands but I spent most of the time looking around me. I'm like my mum, I love reading. We both love stories. For me they opened a world that I could go in and out of safely. But there was so much to look at.

I thought about Daddy and how very brave he was to go in to the forest alone; I couldn't even go with someone. I watched Ben and his friends playing and throwing buckets of water over each other. He had made friends so easily, he always did. There were two boys here that he said were his best friends, Jack and Darren. Today they were playing together right by the water's edge. Water and getting wet seemed to be what they loved best, but they also enjoyed playing cricket or baseball or some kind of football.

Lazily I watched the various other people on the beach; one or two were walking along the edge of the sea; several people were paddling – children with their parents, a group of teenagers, some couples walking and paddling and holding hands. There were families playing games together and quite a few people sitting reading or looking around or sleeping. An older woman, by herself, walked further up the beach kicking up the soft sand with her feet. I enjoyed watching people.

I saw a boy about my own age running along the edge of the water with a dog. He threw a ball and the dog bounded after it and brought it back to the boy. The dog, with the ball in its mouth, was running along with the boy and kept jumping up at him until he took the ball from the dog's mouth and threw it again. The boy had jet black hair and sun-darkened skin. He looked full of health and vitality and something else. What was it? I wondered. I couldn't take my eyes off him, and I realised I had never seen such freedom. That's what it was. He was free.

He came up the beach, running more slowly. He ran past me, the dog jumping at his feet. I watched him as he passed. He stopped and turned. He looked at me, raised a hand and said, "Hey!"

We looked at each other for a few moments, then I raised my hand and said, "Hello." He smiled, took the ball from the dog's mouth, threw it further down the beach, and as the dog hurtled after the ball the boy ran after him.

That was all it was, the first time I saw him, but I was drawn to something in him. I thought about his freedom and confidence. I had always thought of Ben as free. He was wild for sure, but he wasn't free like this boy was free.

six

The next morning when we were out on the balcony having breakfast Ben looked at me and screwed his face up like he did when he was thinking about something he couldn't understand. "Abi," he said. "Why are you frightened of everything?"

I looked down. It was embarrassing having my little brother asking me about it. I felt a bit foolish. I shrugged my shoulders. "I don't really know, Ben. I just am."

"Why do you scream at night?" he asked, still with his face screwed up.

I sighed. He was trying to understand in his own way. "I have dreams that frighten me."

He thought about it for a moment. "Abi, what are you frightened of?"

That was so hard to answer, I didn't really know and I couldn't put it into words very well. "I don't know, Ben. It just feels like something's going to get me."

He looked at me for a while, I don't know what he was thinking. Then very seriously he said "I'm sorry, Abi." He got up and gave me a hug, just like Mum gives him when he's hurt himself. Then he held his arms out to the side and dashed all around the balcony shouting, "I'm

Superman and I'm going to save my sister from the baddies."

As soon as breakfast was finished Ben was itching to get to the beach. He didn't want to do anything else or go anywhere else. He just loved to be playing on the beach with his friends, playing in the sea, playing with a ball.

As soon as we were all ready we went down to the beach again. Ben was playing, Mum and I were reading, as usual. We were quiet and content.

Suddenly something furry was jumping at me and a wet tongue was licking my face. The shock set me screaming and I was completely irrational, it was like my nightmares had just broken into the day. Someone was pulling the animal off me and shouting at it and trying to tell me it wouldn't hurt me. My mum was by my side holding me and talking quietly to me.

"It's just a dog," she said. "It's all right. He's not going to hurt you. It's OK, he's being held. It's OK, Abi, open your eyes and look. It's just a dog, there's a boy holding him. He isn't going to hurt you. He wanted to be your friend. Abi open your eyes."

My eyes were tight shut, I was terrified to look and see whatever it was. I barely heard the words my mother spoke. Or at least I heard them but they didn't make any sense. Then through my screaming and fear I heard a voice full of laughter and concern. It was a strange mixture. It wasn't a "laughing at me" type laughter, more a voice from an ever smiling face, if that makes sense.

"I'm really sorry," it said. "He was bounding up before I realised. He's so friendly. I am so sorry."

I knew immediately it was the voice of the boy I had seen the day before. It seemed to break through all my fears and I stopped screaming. I felt Mum relax and I slowly opened my eyes and looked up. There was the boy standing really close looking at me and holding the dog. He was still smiling but his eyes were deep with compassion.

I looked away, I suddenly felt ashamed of myself. I had often thought how my fearfulness affected my family. But I had never considered how it looked to people generally. How completely ridiculous I probably looked. Then as if he could read my thoughts he said, "It's OK."

He pushed the dog away and told it to sit, and it did. Then he sat down by me and offered me his hand. "Hey, I'm Dominic, most people call me Nic."

"Hi, I'm Abi." And I looked up at him and managed to return his smile.

He offered his hand to my mum and she said, "I'm glad to meet you Nic, I'm Christine."

"You're not cross with me then?" he asked.

"No," she said. "I'm not cross with you."

In all my life I had never felt so at ease with someone so quickly. Meeting new people was always really difficult for me. But Nic was easy to talk to. It wasn't that he did all the talking either. He was really interested in me and my family. Mum just sat back listening as we chattered.

"Are you always afraid of dogs, Abi? Or was it just because Batman leapt at you?"

"Batman?" I asked laughing.

"Oh, there's a story to it, I'll tell you later." He waited.

And I knew what he was waiting for. He wasn't going to let it pass.

"I'm scared of dogs." I replied. "I mean if they keep their distance I don't mind too much. But I don't like to be too close. And anyway I didn't know what it was. He was just on me."

"I'm sorry," he said. And I felt he was more sorry that I was scared of dogs, than of anything else. "Would you like to pat him, if I call him over?"

"No."

"OK."

From the start that's what I liked about Nic. He didn't force an issue. He may have thought it was sad but he kind of accepted what I said and didn't get all pushy. People are often offended if you're scared of their dogs and they try to force you to pat them and see how lovely they really are. But not Nic. He just accepted that I didn't want to.

"Anyway," I said to change the subject, "why did you call your dog Batman?"

He smiled. "Well, he used to be called Dog, boring isn't it? Until the day he flew through the bedroom window with a black cloak, like Batman."

"He did not," I replied.

"He did, I swear it," he replied. "Well, it looked like he flew." I looked doubtfully at him. "I had a black hoodie hanging on my door. He was sniffing around it, then suddenly it fell on top of him, the hood covering his head. He couldn't shake it off, but before I could get it off him he leapt through my bedroom window! He looked just like Batman."

"He could have killed himself," I interrupted.

"He could have, but he didn't," he continued. "He's been called Batman ever since." We sat there for ages chatting and laughing. Nic laughed a lot and I found myself drawn into his world and laughing with him. I was fascinated by him, by his accent, his confidence, his laughter, his energy, his life. He was full of life and loved telling stories. And he loved having an audience.

seven

My mum knew better than to say, "Hey, you've got a little friend". But I could see she was thinking it. It was OK. Grown-ups like to make a big deal of it when you get talking to someone. And I didn't want to talk about it.

But the next morning I was almost as eager as Ben to get on to the beach. And still Mum didn't say anything or make a big deal of it. But she did make every effort to get ready quickly. I didn't have a lot of friends at home. To be honest, I wasn't much fun as a friend in those days, I never wanted to go round their house or do things. Most of the kids at school thought I was a bit freaky and pathetic. There was a girl who was always kind to me, but I was pretty much a loner. So I think Mum was keen to help the friendship along.

Nic had opened a door in my heart. I don't mean I was in love with him or anything like that. No, it was like he had opened a door of friendship, the possibility of friendship without expectations. And there was that freedom and confidence that drew me. I wanted to know him. I wanted to be friends.

We had made no arrangement to meet on the beach the next day, but I hoped. And so we went down to the beach.

All three of us excited. It felt a little strange to be excited, but good, it was not a feeling I was used to. Usually I was too nervous about doing stuff to recognise excitement. I didn't leap around like Ben but I was ready really quickly and even helped wash up the breakfast things.

Ben played ball and splashed about with his friends as usual. Mum read. I held a book in front of my face but I didn't read a word. Every now and again I would raise my eyes above the book and scan the beach. Eventually I saw him, as I hoped I would. Exactly as he had been that first day. Running along the edge of the water, throwing a ball for Batman. When he started running towards me with Batman bounding ahead, fear suddenly started to grip me. I thought for a moment he was just like everyone else and he was going to test me out with his stupid dog. But as he came closer he called the dog, who instantly ran to him. He told him to sit and then came on alone. I breathed again. Not just because I wasn't going to have to face the dog. But because I thought I could trust Nic, and he didn't let me down.

"Hey, Abi," he said.

"Hi, Nic," I replied.

"How are you doin'?"

"I'm fine," I said.

"No. I'm doin' good," he said. I looked at him, confused. "That's what you say in Canada," he explained. "I'm doin' good." I laughed. "Hey, Christine."

"Hey, Nic," she replied. And smiled.

Nic sat down by me. And we looked out to sea, silently. But not an "I don't know what to say" sort of silence. It wasn't awkward. "Have you been anywhere but the beach since you got here?" he finally asked.

"No, mainly stayed around the beach," I replied.

"It's a beautiful place you know. A wonderful place to walk. There's so much to see. Animals, birds, the forest."

"I'm happy on the beach," I replied.

"OK," he said. "Shall I tell you about this place? I've known it all my life."

"Yeah, you can tell me about it."

And he did. He told me of forests, ancient and untouched. Trees that grew so tall and straight you couldn't see the top. He told me of the colours, of the vivid greens. Of trees that had lain fallen for hundreds of years and how new life grew out of them. He told me of shy and elusive wild cats called cougars and how to spot one up a tree; of packs of wolves he had seen when he had been camping in the forest; of his meetings with bears. He told me about the first time he saw a bear by himself when he was camping with his dad.

He had such a respect for the wildlife. As he spoke it came alive. And I, who had always been content to stay in as small a patch of the world as possible, began to feel a stirring deep within me. My father had told me about the wilderness and the animals and shown me pictures in books. It had interested me and I had enjoyed it. But it had not affected me like this. I was beginning to see how completely closed-in my life was. And whilst Nic accepted me as I was, I knew he wanted to stir life in me.

When he stopped talking, we both looked at the sea. We didn't speak for a long time. That was another thing I liked, I didn't feel I had to talk. Except when he asked a question, then he expected to get an answer.

This boy was not like any boy I had ever come across. He was my age. He was the same age as the boys I went to school with. But he was not like them at all. They knew much more about life than I did. But the gulf between them and him was even greater. He had lived in his ten years. I wondered if I had barely been breathing. And yet I knew his kind of life was completely beyond my reach.

"Would you like to go for a walk, Abi ?" he cut right across my thoughts. It took me a moment to think.

"Where?" I asked.

"Not far, just behind the cabins, towards the forest a little way."

"No." I began to panic that he was going to get pushy.

He smiled. "OK. See you." And he stood up, said goodbye to my mum, called Batman and went. All this time Batman had stayed where Nic had left him. They went bounding off together.

eight

All that evening I found myself thinking about Nic. Thinking about the freedom he had. I realised I hardly knew anything about him. Very few facts about him anyway. I didn't know where he lived or who his parents were. I didn't know where he went to school or if he went to school. I guessed he must go to school but he knew so much, I mean about real things. He'd done things and seen things. I don't know what he knew about the kinds of things we learned in school but they didn't seem like they'd be relevant to Nic. And I didn't really know what I meant by that. On the other hand I felt I knew so much about him. I felt I knew something of what made him tick. Mostly I was thinking about the things he had said about this place that had really stirred my heart and brought to life what my dad had only known from books. That got me thinking about my dad. I wondered how he was getting on in the wilderness. I realised how little he knew about the wilderness, how unprepared he was. But I also understood a little more clearly why he wanted to do it.

When I went to bed that night my head was full. I was beginning to feel at peace with the world, I thought to myself. I was beginning to make friends with someone and be interested in something outside of my own world. My own very limited world. The truth that my world was as small as I could make it was really making an impact on me. We had flown thousands of miles from England to the west coast of Canada and I had spent most of my time making sure that I could keep a world around me as tight and small as possible. And there I was making friends with someone whose world seemed to have no boundaries.

Part of me wanted what Nic had. There was a place inside me that longed for the freedom he had, the life he had. But I could not imagine myself in his world, it was a dream, an impossible dream. And also one that terrified me.

That night terror filled me, and even when I was first awake I could not think rationally at all. All I could do was scream and allow Mum to rock me and sing to me. Slowly, very slowly the terror subsided and I began to think clear thoughts. I could not remember such terror and the feeling of its utter reality. Maybe it was because I had got used to life without such nightmares – I had hardly had any since we got here – but I could not completely shake off the sense of the nearness of the terror.

All I could ever remember of my nightmares was that "something" was out to get me. And that "something" had felt very close indeed tonight. Even now it lurked in a corner of my mind. Mum could see that something of the terror was lingering and stayed with me until I eventually went back to sleep.

That morning both Mum and I were tired and ratty.

Ben just ignored our snappiness and got ready to go to the beach. But we were a bit later getting down there than usual. Ben raced off to his friends.

"Let's walk today, Abi," Mum said. I looked at her. "Just along the beach if you like. I feel too restless today to sit and try to read. After last night and expecting Daddy back this evening." I smiled when she said that. I had forgotten for a moment that he was coming home tonight. I thought of all the stories he would have to tell. Not from books this time either. He would have his own experiences to talk about, like Nic.

We didn't usually talk about my nights of terror. Simply because they had happened so frequently there wasn't much to say. But I knew Mum was thinking about it. It had broken through our peaceful days. She was not only restless, she was very quiet and thoughtful. I didn't break in on her thoughts. So we walked silently, up and down the beach. I was content. But I felt that Mum was a bit like a lion in a zoo, pacing. I had put a cage around her as I had with myself. I was safe in mine, she was restless.

We didn't see Nic that day on the beach. I don't know if he was doing something else or if we had missed him because we were late. I was vaguely disappointed. But as the day went on we all began to focus on the fact that Daddy was coming home that night.

nine

"I'm not going to bed," Ben said to Mum. "Not until Daddy gets home."

"He might be very late, Ben. Please go to bed. Daddy will come in to see you when he comes in, however late it is." She was getting frustrated.

"No," said my usually good-natured brother. And there was going to be no shifting him. We had been talking about Daddy coming home all through the afternoon and he wasn't going to miss it now.

"OK," Mum replied wearily. "Come here and I'll read you a story while we wait." Ben ran and got his favourite book of the moment, cuddled into her and we all got absorbed in her reading. My mum was a brilliant reader of stories. She had plenty of practice in the school where she was a classroom assistant. The children loved to hear her read and the teacher would make it a treat for the class. But I think it was Mum who enjoyed it the most. She had a different voice for all the characters and she somehow made them come alive.

It wasn't until she had got to the end of the story that we were all surprised that she had managed to finish it. I think we had thought Daddy would interrupt the story.

Ben was very sleepy and was easily persuaded to go to bed. Mum suggested I should go to bed as well. "I promise I will wake you up the minute he comes in. Abi, it may take Daddy longer to get back from wherever he was going than he thinks. He had no definite plans, just an aim to get home tonight. Go to bed, you can't stay up all night."

I got ready for bed and Mum came to say goodnight. "I'll sit in here until you go to sleep, OK?" I nodded. It was nice to have her safe presence in the room as I lay in bed. I thought about Daddy. For the first time since this morning I thought about Nic. I was sorry I hadn't seen him today. I guess he wasn't likely to hang around someone like me for long. He had too much life and excitement in him and plenty to do.

I awoke to a tapping on my window. My night light was on, as always, so I could see that Mum had gone. I started to panic wondering who, or what, could possibly be knocking on my window late at night. Then I realised it was Daddy. He had got home so late that even Mum had gone to bed and he couldn't get in. It amazes me now how I could possibly have been so stupid and, for me, so brave. I padded across the room and fumbled to open the glass door. I was totally shocked and nearly screamed when I realised it wasn't Daddy at all but Nic.

"Don't scream, Abi," he whispered. He had obviously got to know me quite well already.

"What on earth are you doing here? I would have screamed long ago but I thought it was my dad."

He grinned at me. "I was afraid you might scream."

"What do you want?" I asked again, bewildered, my heart still beating fast, unsure whether I could trust him. This was really weird. Boys don't tap on your window in the middle of the night.

"I want to show you something, Abi."

"Couldn't it wait until the morning?"

"No, it's kind of a night thing." He grinned his mischievous grin at me. "Abi, I want you to trust me. I know you're fearful of lots of things. But I want to show you that it doesn't have to be like that." I began to feel really scared. I didn't want to face my fears, I thought he was going to bring his stupid dog in for me to stroke.

"Nic, I'm fine the way I am. I don't want to stroke your dog."

"It's not the dog." He paused. "Abi, are you scared of the dark?"

"Nic, go away."

"Abi, trust me. I didn't make you stroke the dog, remember? Are you scared of the dark?" I took a deep breath. People tended to avoid talking about my fears. But Nic hit it straight on the head; somehow I wanted to respond to that.

"I'm scared of everything. Yes, I'm scared of the dark. But I can't change it." Nic just accepted that I saw the world in a particular way and he didn't argue with it.

"Abi, there is always a light even in the deepest darkness."

"Is there?" I asked, confused.

"Yes. Can I show you?"

"I don't know. Does it mean turning my night light

off?" Well-meaning family and friends of my parents were always suggesting that they should just turn my night light off and in the end I'd get used to it – but I wouldn't.

"Yes, it does. But that's only so that you can see the light better." He smiled at me again.

"You are a strange person, Nic. OK, you can turn my night light off. If I scream and my mum comes running in here – it's your fault."

"I take the blame." He turned the light off. Panic began to rise. He took me by the hand and led me out to the balcony, I started to pull away. "It's OK," he said. "Look."

I looked about me, I couldn't see a thing. There wasn't a light anywhere.

"I can't see a light," I said in a voice filled with panic.

"That's because you're not looking up." I lifted my head and saw the most dazzling sight. There was the moon shining brighter than I had ever seen it and hundreds and thousands of stars. I had never seen a sky like it. It was utterly beautiful. "There's not much deeper darkness than that, Abi."

"And it's filled with light," I replied. Nic nodded.

"The darker it is around you the brighter you see them."

ten

I awoke to the sun streaming in through my window. The door onto the balcony was closed but the curtains were drawn right back. I remembered Nic's night-time visit and the brilliant light of the moon and the stars. I looked at the open curtains. For a moment I was amazed. I hate to be in a room at night with the curtains open. I hate to look out at the darkness of night. And yet Nic had opened a new world to me – a world of light in the darkness. It's not that I hadn't seen stars before. We have them in our town, but not like that, not so many and so bright. It had been a full moon. And it had been one of the most beautiful things I had seen. And for all its vastness I was not afraid. I wondered about that, but I couldn't understand it. I just remembered being so captivated by the brilliance and the beauty of it that I left my curtains open and fell asleep looking at the moon and the stars.

Suddenly my thoughts changed – Daddy. Daddy must be home. Mum had told me that she would send him in to say hello when he came home. I supposed it had been so late that I was sound asleep and they didn't want to wake me. I leaped out of bed and got dressed as quickly as I could. I had really missed Daddy. I wanted to hear about his adventure, and I wanted to tell him about Nic and about the stars.

When I got into the kitchen Mum was there getting breakfast ready. She was dressed but it didn't look like she had been in bed. And for the first time I had a passing anxiety for my dad. "Is Daddy back?" I asked.

"No." She didn't look at me.

"Have you heard anything?"

"No." She turned to look at me. She looked like she had been crying but she smiled at me. She was trying hard to be cheerful. "Typical Daddy," she said. "Never on time. Couldn't tear himself away from the wilderness. Now could you wake up Ben for me and get him to come and have breakfast?"

"Dad's OK," I said. And I meant it. I just had a deep down feeling that he was all right.

"Yes, yes," she said.

"No, Mum, he is. I'm sure you don't need to worry. I can't explain it, I just have this feeling that's he's fine." She took me in her arms and gave me a big hug.

She seemed more light-hearted at breakfast and seemed to manage Ben's never-ending questions about where Daddy was and why he wasn't home and when would he be home. But she wanted to stay at the house. She wanted to be there when he came home. And I think she wanted to be near the telephone – our mobiles didn't work in Canada.

Ben was a real pain. He was hopeless if he was confined inside for too long, particularly if he didn't have much to do. We exhausted all the games we had very quickly. And I had read to him until we were both tired of hearing my voice.

I didn't mention the previous night and how Nic had shown me the moon and the stars and I had slept with the curtains open. It wasn't that I wanted to be secretive about it. It was just that it was so special to me, I didn't want to spoil it by talking about it.

Sometime mid-morning there was a tap on the door and we all looked at each other. Ben went bounding to the door, Mum and I were close behind. "Oh!" we all said in rather disappointed voices. It wasn't Dad, it was Nic.

"I'm sorry, Nic," I said quickly. "It's not that we're not pleased to see you. It's just that we thought it was my dad."

He came in and we told him about how we had been expecting Dad to come home last night, so now he might walk in any time.

Nic had a wrestling match with Ben on the balcony, Mum and I watched and laughed. Nic had not mentioned his night visit. I thought it was really nice that he realised I might not be ready to talk about it yet.

Nic and Ben lay exhausted on the floor. "Do you want to go to the beach Abi?" Nic asked. "You and Ben could come with me if your mom wants to stay and wait for your dad."

Mum looked at me. I thought for a moment. And then I could feel a smile creeping across my mouth as I realised I could do that. I would feel safe with Nic. He might only have been ten years old but he made me feel safe.

"OK," I said. "If you don't mind being by yourself, Mum."

Mum was almost too shocked to speak. She sat there looking at me. "That's fine," she eventually managed to say. I could tell she desperately wanted to ask me about it. But Mum was always careful not to make too much fuss about what I would and wouldn't do. I think she knew that when I was ready to tell her I would. Anyway it was no big deal really, I simply felt safe with Nic.

We ran down to the beach, Ben chasing Nic. There was Batman, sitting patiently on the beach waiting for Nic. I ground to a halt as I saw him. He began to run towards us but Nic shouted, "Sit!" and he sat just where he was.

"I need to go and explain to Batman. You wait here."

Ben was soon playing with his friends. I told him to stay where I could see him. Batman, as good as gold, stayed where he was, looking a bit sorry for himself. Nic and I walked along the beach barefoot, a safe distance from the sea. Nic said that the only way to walk along the beach was barefoot. "You need to feel the sand between your toes," he said.

All of a sudden he began to run. I stopped and watched him. He looked back at me and shouted over his shoulder, "Come on, Abi!" I still stood and watched. He came running back to me, took my hand and ran with me along the beach. I began to run. I began to feel the wind through my hair, the sand between my toes. I pulled my hand free from Nic and held my arms out to the sides. I began to think I felt like an eagle. I felt like I was flying.

When I stopped I collapsed on the beach laughing, catching my breath. Nic stood by me laughing too.

"That's what it feels like to be free," he said. I looked at him like I didn't know what he meant. But we both knew I did.

eleven

When Ben and I walked back into the cabin at lunch time, Mum took me in her arms and hugged me. When she finally let me go I could see there were tears in her eyes.

"Have you heard anything from Daddy?" I asked.

"No," she said. "But I saw you enjoying yourself." She looked at me. I wondered whether the hug and the tears were about Daddy or me. Probably both.

"It was the best of times; it was the worst of times," she said. I looked at her quizzically. She laughed. "*A Tale of Two Cities*."

"What?" I said.

"It's a book by Charles Dickens," she replied. "The opening line is, 'It was the best of times; it was the worst of times.' That's kind of how today feels." I thought about it but I didn't say anything.

Later in the afternoon when we were all sat on the balcony, Mum brought it up again. "It's the worst of times," she said, "because I do not know where in the world Daddy is. It is the best of times, Abi, because something is happening to you. Something that is almost imperceptible, but you and I know something is different. I'm not asking you to tell me, but I see it."

We were silent for a moment then Ben said cheerfully, "I know where in the world Daddy is, Mummy. He's out there in the forest somewhere." He pointed vaguely. I sighed and gave him a "what a silly little brother" look but Mum laughed. "And he's on his way back," Ben added decidedly.

That evening after Ben was in bed Mum began to pace up and down. I knew that it was becoming almost unbearable for her. I think she didn't feel she could say too much to me. She certainly didn't want to increase any anxiety that I may have had. Poor Mum, she always seemed to have to carry the burden and be strong for everyone else. I decided to go to bed and read so that she could be by herself. Not that I didn't care how she was feeling but so she didn't have to pretend to be cheerful for me. I still had this incredible sense that Daddy was OK. But it's hard to explain that kind of thing to someone else. Maybe that's what Ben had been trying to say.

So I just went up to her, told her I was going to bed and hugged her as she had so often hugged me. "He is all right, Mum." She smiled at me.

"I'll come in, in a while and sit with you as you go to sleep."

"I think I'll be OK," I said. "But you can come anyway if you want."

She did. She kissed me goodnight and said nothing about the fact that the night light wasn't on and the curtains were open.

"Look at the stars, Mum," I said to her. She looked at me quizzically. "Go on, look at them," I encouraged. She walked to the window and looked at the stars and the moon shining so brightly. "Isn't it beautiful," I said. "I've never seen the stars look like that before. Do you know Mum, there's always a light, even in the deepest darkness?"

"Is there?" she asked. "What do you mean?"

I laughed. "I'm not sure, but I know it's true!" She sat near my bed and closed her eyes.

"You know, Abi, I think you're right. I think Daddy is OK. I don't know about light in the deepest darkness. But I think he is all right."

I think we were both surprised to discover me screaming later that night. Mum was there for me, as always. Holding me in her arms and singing. No words, just a beautiful melody. She soothed me with her voice as she had always done, rocking me. I was soothed quicker than usual. But I was sad to discover that the fears were still there.

In the morning I found Mum preparing breakfast. She looked less weary than the previous day and looked like she had slept, at least some of the night.

"I'm sorry, Mum."

"Whatever for, Abi?"

"For screaming last night. That my nightmares haven't stopped."

"Darling, don't be silly," she said. "I have gone to you in the night nearly all your life. And I'll do it for as long as you need me. But you know what? Last night, I began to believe it won't be for ever."

twelve

Mum rang the Search and Rescue people that morning. They wanted her to call into their office as soon as possible, so she could take them some photos of Daddy and tell them anything she knew about where he might have gone. She made arrangements for Ben to spend the day with friends, who would have looked after me as well but I would rather go with Mum than be left with people I didn't know. She was relieved when she saw Nic walking up the beach to our cabin and asked me if I would stay with Nic if he didn't mind. I was reluctant but agreed and Nic was fine with that too.

I was scared of being left without Mum in calling distance, but I kept reminding myself that I was safe with Nic, I trusted Nic.

We had a gentle morning. Roaming around on the beach, looking in the rock pools. Nic knew so much about the wildlife. He knew the names of the sea anemones and the fish and the different kinds of weed. He pointed out all the different birds that flew over and the songs we could hear. I was captivated by it all.

It was as we were walking back to the cabin for lunch that I plucked up the courage to ask what had been on my mind for the last couple of days. "Nic, what did you mean about there always being a light even in the deepest darkness? I mean I understand about the stars and the moon shining in the night and the darker it is around you, the brighter you see them. But you thought it would help me not to be afraid, and it's not just the dark I'm afraid of."

"Well," he replied, "it's like the moon and stars are a picture of another kind of light. It's always there. Whether it's darkness or just that life feels dark, this light is always shining. It's just a matter of knowing how to look."

"And how do you look?"

"Well, that's something you kind of have to discover."

"I don't know what you mean."

"Maybe I can show you something tonight."

"Maybe," I said.

Mum came back after lunch. They were going to give it another night. If Daddy hadn't shown up by tomorrow morning they would begin searching. The Search and Rescue people apparently didn't think that Daddy would have got too far and that finding him, they hoped, would not be too difficult. Mum said they were a bit rude about people going into the forest unprepared.

She was edgy and impatient that afternoon. She couldn't settle to anything. She'd walk along the beach for a few minutes and then want to go back in. She would pick up a book but I don't think she would read a word that made any sense and then she would lay it down again. She made endless cups of coffee, I had never seen her drink so much coffee. Her edginess began to affect me.

"Will you please go and do something, Abi? You don't need to be hanging around with me. Nic, will you take Abi to the beach? You just make me more nervous," Mum said sharply. I was stung by her impatience and that she wanted to get rid of me. I understood why, but my own increasing anxiety, fuelled by hers, made me reply crossly.

"I don't want to go to the beach. Nic isn't my baby-sitter."

Mum was about to reply equally as snappily. But Nic cheerfully took me by the hand and dragged me away. When we were out of the cabin he said, "You're just winding each other up."

We were walking towards the sea. When I was aware of what we were doing I stopped. The sea was far too big and wild for me. Nic carried on until he reached the edge of the tide. He turned towards me and beckoned me to him. For some reason that gesture made me really cross. I suddenly felt like his little "project". I had liked Nic from the start because he didn't make me do things I didn't want to do and he didn't seem to have expectations. But as I stood there looking at him calling to me to come closer to the sea, I could see he had succeeded in making me do a number of things I had never done before and without my even realising. I felt cross. If I wasn't so afraid of being on the beach alone I would have stomped off. But I wasn't sure he would come after me. And suddenly even the beach seemed huge and I felt afraid. So, frustratingly, I burst into tears instead!

Nic walked slowly towards me. I was grateful he didn't run to me and make me feel more of a baby than I already felt. "I'm sorry," he said. "I didn't mean to make you cry. I just . . ." he ran out of words.

So I finished the sentence for him. "You just thought you'd try and encourage me to do what I'm afraid of because you think you're my teacher or something. Well, you're not," I shouted at him.

"No," he replied. "I don't think I'm your teacher, I thought I was your friend. Friends encourage each other, I thought." He was hurt but he wasn't cross.

"Well, if you're my friend just accept me the way that I am!" I was still shouting, I could barely help myself, but a part of me wanted to hurt him, like I felt he'd hurt me.

"I do," he said. "I do accept you just the way you are. That's not the point. Because I'm your friend I want you to see that there is a whole lot more to life than you are living."

"I know that!" I sobbed. "Do you think I don't realise? But I can't change!"

"You can." My anger didn't bother him one little bit. And suddenly it vanished.

I felt exhausted. And I cried, but they were different tears than before, those had been tears of self-pity and frustration. I don't know what these tears were, but they were from a different place. Grief maybe, for a wasted life, genuine fear for my dad, sorrow that I had hurt my friend. I don't know. But Nic waited.

Finally I was through and I looked at Nic. He smiled sheepishly, probably not used to girls' tears. "Sorry," he said. "Life has risk in it, Abi. If it doesn't, it isn't really life. Your dad took a risk in going into the forest, but he needed to do it. Do you think he wasn't afraid? Of course he was afraid. Your mom took a risk in letting him go. Do you think she wasn't afraid? They both took a risk in coming here with you. Sometimes life is risky. There are foolish risks and there are risks that you've just got to take. You have to learn that, Abi. If you are ever to give yourself a chance at life you are going to have to let yourself take a risk. And we're not talking huge, major risks here." I was about to shout again, but he cut in. "No, don't shout at me. I know how hard it is for you. And I am not going to make you do anything."

We sat silently for a long while. For a ten-year-old boy he was very good at silence. Eventually I stood up and slowly, slowly began to walk towards the sea. It is hard to understand, I know, but I was terrified of the immensity of it. I took a few paces and I looked back. Nic was still sitting where I had left him.

"Well, do I have to do this by myself," I asked, "or would my friend like to come with me?" He laughed. Together we walked to the sea. We didn't talk.

I stood at the shoreline watching wave after wave come in, wondering why ever was I doing this? Nic encouraged me to take off my flip-flops and let the sea cover my feet.

"How does it feel?" he asked.

"Awful," I said.

"Why?"

"Because it is so big and I am so small."

But I survived. And that is what I kept thinking. I survived, every wave. It didn't swallow me up. I am still here.

thirteen

I do not know how I let him persuade me. I could hardly believe it was me. It really did feel as if I was watching someone else. But here we were, walking away from the beach, away from the cabin, towards the forest. We were walking along a sandy track that wound around our group of cabins, through some trees, to the road. We walked in silence. That was another thing I liked about Nic – he didn't expect you to explain everything. He seemed to understand that not everything could be put into words. Not that I was thinking of anything deep. All I was focussing on was putting one foot in front of the other. Carrying me further away from safety. And yet beyond that I realised that I was doing it; nobody was making me walk, I was choosing to do it. I had never gone anywhere without my parents, further away, or more dangerous, than school. And even that was a trauma every morning.

As we put the cabin behind us we turned down a straight road, with trees and bushes becoming thicker on either side as we walked further away from the beach. Gradually the familiar sound of the sea faded. It felt as if the trees were soaking up the sound. The gentle lapping of the waves had filled every moment since we got here;

it had become familiar and safe, even while the sea itself was big and uncertain. Now, as we walked on, the forest became increasingly dark and thick until the trees were huge. In reality we were only on the edges of the forest, but to me it looked mysterious and scary, so I tried to look straight ahead. I could see mountains tops in the distance but you couldn't avoid the trees. The road was straight. It wasn't a busy road but there was a small steady flow of cars and a few other walkers. I felt vaguely amazed that no one stopped us and asked what we were doing or where we were going. Then I realised that it was "normal". No one could see anything odd about two kids walking down the road. I wanted to shout out, "I've never done anything like this before, I don't go anywhere without my parents and then not without a big fuss," but I remained silent. For a moment I felt elated, I wanted to run. But almost in that instant I suddenly felt terrified. I couldn't do it. I stopped.

"Where are we going?" I asked Nic in a panicky voice.

He glanced at me and just said, "You know where we're going."

"Tell me where we're going. I don't think I can do it." I was beginning to feel sick and the ground seemed to be less firm than it had been.

Calmly Nic told me we were going to the rainforest. "There's a boardwalk around part of it. It's for tourists, but you get a feel of the forest. Its ancientness. You'll be fine. But we can go back any time you want to. Do you want to go back now?" He looked straight at me. He wasn't challenging me exactly, but there was something in his eyes. I knew I could go back and he would think none the worse of me, but, what was it? He truly wanted me to do it. And he believed I could do it. That was what I saw in his look. I continued to try to focus on putting one foot in front of the other.

"What is a boardwalk?" I asked him peevishly.

"It's just a path through the forest that's boarded – boardwalk, see." I managed a small laugh. "It's like a nature trail," he continued. "It does a small circle round a bit of the forest. You're never that far from the road. But it's neat if you've never been in the forest before."

"I thought rainforests were in really hot places, like the Amazon, I've seen on TV," I said. I was worrying about the small creatures that might be there as well as the big ones.

"They are," he replied. "That's tropical rainforests. This is a temperate rainforest. It doesn't get really, really hot but it rains a lot. We get a lot more rain than this usually."

I started walking again. I have no idea how long it took us. Probably no more than ten minutes. But we arrived at the start of the boardwalk.

"Abi," he said seriously, "you won't ever have been anywhere like this in your life."

"I know," I said, too loudly.

"Now if we want to have a chance to see any wildlife you'll have to be quiet. Move quietly, speak quietly. And don't scream if you see something."

"But my dad said that you were supposed to make noise to scare off the animals."

"Well, for a greenhorn that's the best," he said smiling widely.

"What's a greenhorn?" I asked.

"Someone who's new to the wilderness," he replied.

"I'm a greenhorn," I said, again too loudly.

"But I'm not and it would be really neat for you to see something like a bear or a cougar, or a wolf. I know what to do. I've been coming to the forest all my life. You'll be fine. It would be really neat for you to see that these animals are not out to get you. But even if we don't see any animals it's a wild place."

"Nic, you're scaring me."

"You're scared anyway, remember?" And he laughed, loudly. I frowned.

"I don't think my fearfulness is a thing for you to laugh at! And you're scaring me. I don't want to see a wild animal, a grizzly bear or something."

"Oh that's OK. There aren't any grizzlies here." I looked at him, he was serious.

"But my dad said there was and that you play dead if you see one."

"OK, your dad knows more about Vancouver Island than me, right? No, we only have black bears, believe me. And you don't play dead with a black bear. You act aggressive and you don't scream."

"Well I never liked the idea of playing dead anyway. But I make no guarantees about screaming. I'm a good screamer."

"I'm serious, don't you scream."

He was beginning to annoy me. As if I had any control over my screaming. But I was getting nervous and in no mood for an argument. I was excited but I was more scared. "Let's get on with it," I said.

He was right. I had never been anywhere like this in my whole life. And for a moment I stopped thinking about my fear and looked in awe all around me. The green was vivid. Quietly Nic was giving me a running commentary of the trees and plants and the birdsong and the flowers. It was like quiet music being played in the background. I barely took on board the actual words but captured something of his respect and his knowledge and his love for this place. It was magnificent. He told me how some of the trees that had fallen on the ground had lain there for hundreds of years and had been alive for hundreds of years before that. What struck me most was the life that was teeming in this place, life everywhere, life growing out of the decay. Old trees lay rotting with new trees and ferns growing out of them. I mentioned this to Nic.

"Yes," he said, "that's the way of life here in the rainforest. Death becomes life for something else."

I looked at him. It sounded odd but it sounded deep too.

"You know Nic," I said very quietly. "I've never really thought about God before, and I don't know if I believe in him. But I almost think I could, being here." Nic nodded and smiled.

We walked quietly for a little while. One or two people had walked past us, but we were alone now. We stopped and looked and listened. There was gentle birdsong. The sounds were light and soft; melodic tweeters and humming insects. We saw birds flitting up in the trees. He pointed out the tiniest little brightly coloured hummingbird. It was all a more simple beauty than the boldness I had expected. It was the colours of the place that were the really amazing thing, mostly the many different colours of vivid green. There were some big, bright flowers, purples, oranges. We listened and we looked. I was scared but I tried to focus on the beauty around me.

"Hey, hey, hey," he said in a tiny whisper and took hold of my arm. "Now do exactly as I tell you."

"What is it?" I said, panic rising.

"Don't scream. Look between those trees as far as you can look," and he pointed.

"I can't see anything. I want to go, I'm scared," and I began to breathe very loudly, stifling a scream. "Take me home."

"You're going to have to wait." He had a very firm hold of my arm.

"You said I could go back when I liked." Panic was filling me.

"Now's not a good moment, you're going to have to wait. Look again. Can you see something black?" He was gentle, his voice was soothing, but it was firm and I knew he was serious about me staying put and not screaming. "It's a bear." He sounded almost gleeful! I looked and I began to make it out. A scream rose to my throat. Close into my ear Nic whispered firmly, "Shut up! He's seen us, he's watching us. If you act scared he is more likely to attack. Enjoy this sight. They are beautiful animals. You don't get to see them often."

The bear began to amble towards us. My heart stopped, I'm sure. Life stopped. I didn't dare release the scream I longed to scream. My eyes were riveted on the bear. I felt rather than saw Nic pick up a stick. He whispered in my ear to back away with him. The bear looked at us then turned and walked away. I began to breathe. And tears rolled down my face. Nic looked at me and chuckled. "That was cool," he said, "I reckon it was a gift from the God you've just begun to believe in."

"What? That we've escaped with our lives?" I said between sobs.

"No," he laughed, "for you to see a bear like that. Hey, and you didn't scream."

"I'd have been more scared of you than the bear, if I had," I snapped, wiping the tears from my face with my hands. "Why did it walk away like that, why didn't it attack us?"

"Because they don't live just to attack people. That's not how they get their fun. They usually only attack people if they're scared. They don't eat people, you know. They eat dandelions, mostly."

"Ha, ha," I replied

"It's true. How are you feeling, anyway?"

"I don't know. Shaky, but OK. I survived. Like the sea. I didn't get swallowed up. That's all I ever remember of my nightmares – something is out to get me, to swallow me up. This place is vast, the sea is vast and I always feel so small and afraid. But it feels sort of vast but OK."

"You took a risk, and you're OK. That's good."

fourteen

"Where have you been, Abi?" Mum asked as soon as I walked in the door. "I couldn't see you on the beach."

"I've just been walking with Nic. He's been showing me things. He knows this place so well."

"He lives here, Abi."

"Yeah, but I don't know much about where I live," I replied.

"No." Mum came over and hugged me. She didn't say anything just hugged me. And I knew she was crying. My brave mother, was weeping in my hug. She had been, understandably, distracted since my dad went away. And I had not been so dependent on her for my own reasons. She had been my strength all my life and now she needed some strength, and for the first time ever I felt I had a tiny bit of strength to give another person. All this went through my mind as we hugged.

"I haven't been there for you like usual, have I, Abi. I'm sorry. But I feel like you're working some things out."

It wasn't a question, just an indication that she could see more than I thought she could see and she was giving me an opportunity to talk if I wanted to. But I didn't. Not yet. I felt like something was happening to me and I couldn't put words to it yet. I was silent.

Eventually I just said, "I feel more like some things are working out me." I didn't really understand what I meant, myself.

My ever-patient, accepting mother smiled and let it pass. We sat silently, each deep in thought. Suddenly our thoughts were jolted by the telephone. We looked at each other and Mum rushed to answer it.

"Hello," I heard her say anxiously. Then her tone changed completely as she endeavoured to be polite. "Oh hello, is Ben OK?" Pause. "No, I think I'd like him to come home. Thank you so much for taking care of him today." Pause. "No, we haven't heard anything yet. OK, thank you again, goodbye."

She sighed deeply as she put the receiver down. Then she began to laugh. I looked up at her, surprised. "I am so tense," she said. And then she began to cry again, "Do you still say that Daddy's OK, Abi?"

"Yes, Mum, I do. I don't know why. I just feel it. He's working some things out too. There's something about the wildness of this place that makes you do that."

Our peace was shattered moments later by a whirlwind on two legs! My brother came hurtling in followed by his friend's mother. The two mothers chatted in hushed tones at the door while Ben told me everything he had done all day, in two minutes flat.

"Is Dad back yet?" he finally found space enough to ask.

"No," I replied.

"Oh," he said, "I want to tell him about the runs I

scored this morning. Is he going to be back soon?"

"Yes," Mum said as she came back into the room. "I think he will be."

"Mum?" I said, not quite knowing how to put what I had been thinking since Nic and I were walking back from the rainforest. I hesitated.

"Yes," she prompted.

"Well . . . Could we pray?"

"Pray?" she sounded surprised.

"For Daddy."

She looked at me strangely but was smiling. "Do you know how to pray?"

"No, well, I think we've done it in school assembly sometimes. Not really." I laughed nervously to cover my embarrassment. "Do you?"

She shook her head. "No, not really."

"Can we try?" I persisted.

"If you want to. It can't do any harm. Where's all this come from?"

"I don't know really. I just would like to, all of us together."

"I know how to pray," said Ben.

"How do you know how to pray?" I asked.

"One of my friends at school prays sometimes and his mum and dad pray at tea. You say, dear God, this is Ben. Help my daddy. Amen."

"You start then, Ben," I said.

"I've done it. It's your turn."

I felt foolish but Ben made it look so simple. "OK. Dear God, this is Abi. Please look after Daddy. Amen."

"Amen," Ben said loudly. "Now you, Mummy."

Mum looked at me, then closed her eyes. "Dear God, this is Christine. Please bring Dave, Daddy, back to us. Amen."

"Amen," Ben and I said together.

Mum and I had both felt a bit foolish, but not Ben. It seemed such simple words. But we had meant it.

fifteen

We went to bed a little deflated that night. We had still not heard anything from Daddy; somehow after we had prayed we sort of expected to. And a little later we heard from the Search and Rescue people who said they would begin searching for Daddy at first light in the morning if they heard nothing from us beforehand. It seemed to make it feel like there was really something wrong. But underneath the anxiety I had for Daddy, for some unaccountable reason I still believed he was OK. He might need finding, but he was OK.

I lay awake a long time, thinking. Thinking about all that had happened over the last few days. Daddy going off so excited and then not returning when we expected him. I thought about my friendship with Nic and the amazing things he had encouraged me to do. No one, not even my parents, had ever been able to persuade me to do what I was too afraid to do: I had never slept without a light before; I had never been in the sea; stroked a dog; been for a walk anywhere far with, or without, my parents. Now I had been into the sea. I had walked in the rainforest and seen a bear without screaming! I had seen the stars without any other light around and now I slept without a night light because there is always a light even in the deepest darkness. Even though I didn't know what that meant, it comforted me and I believed it.

And I thought about Nic. In some ways I knew very little about him. The ordinary everyday kinds of chit chat had never really come into our conversation. I still didn't know where he lived, what his surname was, who his parents were, where he went to school. But I felt I knew him so well and I trusted him. I wasn't used to friendship. I got along by myself at school and never visited anyone. I never went to parties. My world had always consisted of Mum, Daddy and Ben.

And so I lay awake thinking. I was fully alert when I heard a knocking on my window. I was alarmed until I remembered that night when Nic had visited me and showed me the stars. Then I heard him whispering and began to make out his face peering in. I laughed and went and opened the door.

"Why don't you use the front door like everyone else?" I whispered. "It's OK, I see the moon and the stars every night now. I sleep with the curtains open."

He came in. "That's great!" he replied. "Can I show you something else tonight? I was going to mention it before but I wasn't sure with your dad and everything. We may not have another chance and I really want to show you real darkness."

"Tonight? Now? I thought this was real darkness."

He grinned for a reply.

"Where?" I asked.

"The rainforest," he replied.

I laughed and quickly stopped myself, I didn't want to wake Mum up. "Nic, there's a million reasons why I can't come traipsing off to the rainforest with you in the middle of the night. I never go out at night, the rainforest was challenge enough in the daylight, I would scream at night – you just plain wouldn't get me there. I can't go out without telling Mum, and she wouldn't let me go."

"Don't ask, just come. I know, really, you should ask," he looked a bit guilty. "But she wouldn't understand and you'll be back before she knows you're not here. You've said before you couldn't do things and every time you've been able to."

"Nic, this is silly." I was lost for words, I couldn't believe that Nic would ask me to do something so completely stupid. "It's totally ridiculous." But he just looked at me like he knew I would change my mind. I thought of screaming so that my mum would come running and tell him to go away and not be so stupid. But I didn't. Somehow I couldn't.

"You'll need to wear something fairly warm," was all he said.

"I'm not going," I said.

He looked at me for a moment. "OK," he said. And he turned back to the glass door and began to leave. Half way out he stopped and said, "I just thought you wanted to know about the light that shines even in the deepest darkness."

I watched him and I knew I would have to go with him. "All right," I said. "I'll come. Wait for me outside while I get changed."

Minutes later I was outside standing next to Nic, wishing I had never met him, wishing he would leave me alone, wishing I was back in bed, wishing that Daddy was home. Terrified.

We walked in silence. I kept looking at the moon. "Light in the deepest darkness," I kept saying to myself. The sky was so clear and the moon so bright that it really was quite easy to see. I began to relax as I thought about the afternoon and that I had been there before and I had survived.

As we walked into the rainforest the light of the moon began to fade. And we stood in darkness I could not have imagined. Slowly my nightmares seemed to envelope me. I knew that something lurked in this place, maybe worse than a bear, that would get me. The years of waking up in terror with only a vague memory that something was trying to get me flooded back, and regardless of everything, I screamed with terror. The darkness was so deep and I could see nothing. There was no light. There was only fear and darkness and "something". I turned to run but Nic grabbed me. I lashed out at him but he just held firmly onto my arms.

"Let me go," I screamed. "Let me go!"

"It's OK," he said. I was sobbing loudly. "Scream if you want. There's nothing going to hurt you. You're not scared of bears, are you? I mean not in particular. You're scared of life, you're scared of being alone. But you're not alone."

My sobbing began to subside. I whimpered. I felt like an animal must feel when it's been caught in a trap and it has thrashed around until all its energy has vanished and it waits quietly to see what will happen.

Nic moved away from me. For a moment the panic began to rise again, I couldn't see him. "What are you doing? Where are you going?" I asked.

"It's all right, I'm still here. I'm just giving you some space."

"I don't want space. There's too much space. I'd rather you stayed right by me where I can feel you."

"It's OK, I'll keep talking. I'm going to tell you about the light in the deepest darkness. I can feel light all around me. Can you, Abi?"

"No," I replied desperately. "I sort of expect to see light not feel it."

"It's a light that I carry, a presence that I carry really." He paused for a moment. "You have lived all your life in darkness. And the only way you've found to cope with that is to try to control it, to make it as small as possible. But you can't control it Abi. The darkness is vast. This place is vast and it's just a picture of how vast the darkness is. Darkness is everywhere, all around. No matter how hard you try you can't make it small enough to live with. Does it sound hopeless?"

Did it sound hopeless? Whatever was he trying to say to me? I could feel him smiling.

He continued, "You have to be filled with light, that way no matter where you go, there's light. You can't change the darkness but you can carry light, and where that light is there isn't any darkness."

Suddenly Nic flashed his torch on. There wasn't a lot of light but he was right, where it shined there was no darkness.

"So all this is to tell me to carry a torch all the time?" I asked. I sounded unimpressed I'm sure, but really I was captivated. The torch went out.

"No," he replied, "batteries run out." I think he was trying to be funny. "Do you remember we talked of God earlier?"

I was suddenly jolted. "God?" I said out loud. I was nervous. I had been toying with the idea of God for a day or two but I didn't want Nic to talk to me about God. I don't know what I had expected, but not God! I wanted something concrete and real, something that I could see.

"Yeah, God. You said you were beginning to believe in Him."

"Yeah, but he's some distant being that made all this and watches on isn't he? He's not interested in whether I'm scared or not. We prayed this evening, Mum and Ben and me. For Daddy to come home, but it didn't work."

"How do you know it didn't work? How do you know God isn't answering it right now, showing your dad how to get home? Just because it didn't happen within five minutes, doesn't mean it isn't going to. And God is interested in you and your fearfulness. That's your answer, Abi. God. Jesus. He made light and he is light. Walk with Jesus and there is always light even in the deepest darkness. He does care, for you, for me. I know, I walk in his light." With that he took my arm and turned me around. "Come on," he said, "we'd better get back."

"That's it," I said, disappointed. "Walk with this God of yours and I'll always have light?"

"Yeah," he said simply.

"Are you going to try to persuade me to believe?"

"No," he said.

We walked in silence for a while.

"Why not?" I finally asked.

"Because you have a brain to think with and God is more able to do his own persuading than I am."

"Maybe I need some more information."

"Maybe you need to listen to what you've already heard, with the heart that God gave you. I've told you what I know and what you need to hear. Now it's your choice."

sixteen

When we got back to the cabin, all the lights were on. I suddenly felt scared. I knew that Mum had discovered I was missing and she would be tearing her hair out. She would be really scared and really angry. I felt sick. I looked at Nic. He understood what I was thinking.

"Do you want me to come in with you?" he asked. "It's kind of my fault."

"No, I'd better go in by myself. But don't worry, I'll blame you!"

He smiled.

There didn't seem much point in climbing up my balcony so I went to the front door. It was unlocked. I walked in. I turned to see Nic watching me, I waved and shut the door.

The house was in uproar. The phone was ringing; Mum was shouting; Ben was screaming; and Daddy calmly answered the phone. I did a double-take – Daddy! Suddenly I forgot the terrible trouble I was going to be in, everything was fine, Daddy was back! I ran to him, shouting, "Daddy, Daddy."

As I threw myself around him, Daddy hugged me with one arm and held the phone with the other. I heard him say, "Um, I'm sorry but it looks like we need to cancel that report of a missing person, she's here." He listened. "Yeah, it looks like she's fine." Pause. "Thank you. Yes it looks like we're all back together again. Goodnight, sorry to have put you to so much trouble. Goodnight."

He put down the phone, slowly it seemed to me. He looked at me, tears were running down his face, "Where in the world have you been Abi? You terrified us."

"So did you, Daddy," I replied. He laughed. I snuggled into him so very pleased to have him back.

"She's back," Dad yelled above the noise, as he held me to himself.

Instantly Mum stopped shouting and Ben stopped screaming. I looked up, Ben and Mum's faces were a picture of disbelief and shock. She didn't even have the energy to shout, she just came up and took me from my dad and held me, sobbing. Eventually she was able to speak.

"Why ever did you run off, Abi? Now you're back safe and sound, I don't know whether to be really angry with you for frightening me like that or pleased that you had the courage to go off! Oh Abi, what has been going on? I've missed something!"

But I found I only had one thing to say. I didn't want to defend myself or explain anything right now.

"But, Mum, Daddy's home. We prayed and Daddy's come home."

"Yes, darling, Daddy's home. I don't know if it had anything to do with us praying, but he's home and that's all that matters."

"Is it?" I thought. "Is it all that matters? Does it matter whether God answered or if it's coincidence?" Ben interrupted my thoughts:

"Can I hug you, Abi?"

"Of course you can."

"I'm really glad you're back," he said as he squeezed me tightly. "And that Daddy's back."

My mum decided that as all the "adventurers" were back safe and sound she would make some hot chocolate and we could each tell our stories. I was hesitant to talk of my experiences, I still felt I needed to think about it all. I didn't really know what I thought about any of it. And I was so excited that Daddy was back that I wanted to hear him. And Ben didn't think I would have anything much to say, he would much rather hear about Daddy's adventures in the wilderness.

We sat around drinking hot chocolate, strangely quiet. We were all tired, though none of us wanted to go to bed. Ben and I wanted to hold on to Daddy for as long as possible, afraid he would disappear again if we went to bed. Daddy was desperately tired and didn't seem much more able to talk about his adventures than I was. Mum had felt so many things over the past few days and had tried so hard to hold it together. She just sat on the sofa with my daddy, clinging hold of him. I sat on her lap, Ben sat on Daddy's. Mum kept looking at us both and smiling. No energy to talk, no desire to go to bed. And we sat like this long into the night.

Eventually Mum was sound asleep in Daddy's arm and I was fighting following her. I could distantly hear Ben still chattering away, telling Daddy all he had been up to. He seemed to have decided that he had obviously had the most exciting time of all of us and was quite content to talk all night about it.

Then I heard Daddy whisper to me that it was time to go to bed. He gently lay Mum on the sofa and carried me into my room. He tucked me into my bed, in my clothes and kissed me goodnight.

"Maybe you and I will be able to tell of our adventures in time." He switched my night light on and turned the main light off. That stirred something in me.

"No, Daddy, I don't have the night light any more. Can you open the curtains so that I can see the moon and the stars?"

He looked at me in surprise, but did what I asked and left. I fell asleep instantly.

seventeen

When I woke up I wondered why I felt so excited. Then I remembered Daddy was home. I began to ask myself the question, "Was it God? Did he bring Daddy back because we prayed? Does it matter?" It did matter to me. For some reason it mattered very much.

I began to remember the other events of yesterday evening – going to the rainforest with Nic. Was there really a God who cared about me? A God who cared about my fears, who cared enough to fill me with light? Nic had said something about walking with Jesus – what did that mean? How do you "walk with Jesus"? I remembered him telling me how I never need be alone. Is that what it meant to walk with Jesus? Like going everywhere with him? "Is that the kind of God you are?" I asked out loud. "The kind of God who would let me kind of hang out with you?" I laughed, it seemed outrageous.

"Are you all right, Abi?" Mum asked as she walked into my room. "I thought I heard you talking."

"I'm fine," I replied. "I'm not sure if I've ever felt better."

Mum looked at me with a big smile. "You know, Abi, you look better than I've ever seen you. Maybe it's just all the fresh air you've had but, I don't know." She hesitated. "Abi, can I ask you a question?"

I nodded.

"Why did you go off last night?"

I thought for a while. I didn't know how to answer. I'm not even sure I understood myself why I agreed to go off with Nic in the middle of the night without telling anyone. "I don't know, Mum. I didn't want to make you worried, though I knew it would. I just had to do it. I was with Nic – please don't be cross with him."

"I'm not cross any more," she said. "But I was so frightened. Daddy came home and I was so relieved and we came in here to tell you and you were gone. What was I supposed to think? My little Abi who never goes anywhere, who's afraid of her shadow, going off in the middle of the night. I get one back and lose another!" She hugged me. "Are you going to tell me what's going on?"

"I need to think, Mum. I need to think something through and then I'll tell you about it."

"You and your daddy are so alike. He's also finding it hard to put into words."

As soon as breakfast was over I went for a walk, by myself, along the beach. When I mentioned it to my parents they laughed. They looked so relaxed and happy together.

For the first time in my entire life I was walking alone. And I felt like I could breathe. I stood for a while just taking in deep breaths. How strange it was that I should suddenly feel able to breathe having never been aware that I was not able to breathe. All of a sudden I spread my arms out like wings and ran as fast as I could. I had such a sense of freedom. I felt like a bird that has spent all its life in a cage and is suddenly set free. I had, in my own strange way, been content with my restricted life because I knew no different but now the cage seemed to be opened and there was a whole world to fly in. I stopped running and looked towards the sea. It was scary, my world expanding so much, so quickly. I walked down to the edge of the tide, I didn't paddle, I just made myself look at the hugeness of it. "Well, God," I said, "I don't know if I ever thought about you much before, but ever since I met Nic it's like you've been after me, maybe before, maybe you're the reason we're here at all. I don't even know if I have much to think about, I don't know if you're letting me think about it. You've been showing me wonderful things and showing me you care. And I don't care if anyone says it's a coincidence that Daddy came back after we prayed. Maybe you arranged Nic and all of it. Whatever it means to 'walk with Jesus', I want to. I want to hang out with you, so that I'm never alone and there's always a light in the deepest darkness." And I sat on the sand and laughed and laughed with a freedom I had never known.

eighteen

That afternoon, after lunch, the four of us sat on the balcony, quietly, almost shy of each other it seemed. It was time to tell our stories. Daddy began. He told us how he started out boldly, but also told us of his fear. He soon realised he was not well prepared for wild country. He made us laugh as he re-enacted his first night all by himself in the wilderness, sleeping in his tent. He had hung his food in a tree a long way from his tent to keep bears from bursting into his tent. That was what everyone had said to do. But it didn't make him any easier. He didn't sleep a wink. Every noise he heard terrified him and he was sure he would never live to see daylight again. He told us about the birds and plants and animals he saw, always on edge in case he came across a bear. He rang his bear bell loudly all the time and his hand kept going to his can of bear spray fixed to his belt. But in all his time out in the wilderness he never did see a bear. I laughed. Everyone looked at me. Daddy raised his eyebrows but I just told him to carry on.

"What's a bear bell, Daddy? Is it a bell a bear wears?" asked Ben.

"No, Tigger. It's this little bell here," he took it out of

his pocket and showed us. You put it on your belt or carry it and ring it. That way the bears know you're coming and keep out of your way. Or you can sing while you walk. I should have tried it."

"That would have scared the bears, Daddy," Ben said.

"That would be cruelty to wildlife," Mum added.

"Enough rudeness!" Daddy said, pretending to be hurt, but his eyes twinkled.

"What's bear spray, Daddy?" I asked.

"It's a pepper spray. If you're attacked by a bear you're supposed to spray it in its eyes and it'll blind it for a short while, to give you time to run, you've got to run fast. You have to let it get really close to aim right. If you don't, you just end up making it angry. Not good having an angry bear after you."

It was when he spoke of his loneliness and fear of failing, not just in the wilderness, but in life, I became really gripped. Mum didn't understand.

"But you have made it in life, Dave! You've got a good family and a good job. In what way haven't you made it?" she asked.

"I don't think I can explain. I just haven't ever been sure I had what it took. I don't know how long I've consciously thought that, but somewhere it's lurked inside. I'm not asking you to understand. I'm just telling you the way it was . . . is. I wanted to see the wildlife and experience the wilderness. There's nowhere in Britain you can truly do that. But it was more than that, I had to do it. Just me against the elements I guess. Maybe we were made for wilderness; life in Britain is safe and tame. The wildest it gets in England is at a football match on a Saturday afternoon."

"That's pretty wild," Mum admitted with a smile. Daddy laughed.

"This sounds awfully deep and meaningful but it didn't feel like that at the time. It was an adventure, a journey. Anyway I got completely and utterly lost. I tried to follow trails but they branched off so often. I tried to make markers but I never seemed to be able to find them again. I got so scared I started to pray!"

Ben and I looked at each other and smiled.

"I had been wandering around for a couple of days, desperate. And, like I said, I started praying. But it wasn't until yesterday evening I had any hope of ever finding my way out. It was early evening and I was really wanting to lie down and die. I was willing you to get the Search and Rescue people out, then I began to see a light. I hadn't been able to see the light of the stars or the moon most of the time I had been in there. Mostly it's too dense. First of all I thought I was dreaming but it seemed real. I didn't know if it was the moon, but I made for it because, even if it was only a clearing where the moon was shining, it might mean I was getting to an edge somewhere. I followed it for a while and suddenly I came out onto a road. I couldn't see any light but I was certainly glad to get out. I started walking north. I had no idea where I was, but it seemed like a good idea. I walked for a while and when a truck came by, I flagged him down and he brought me back here."

We were all silent. I don't know what Mum was

thinking but I was certainly connecting Daddy's light with the fact that we had prayed yesterday evening. Ben suddenly perked up and said, "We prayed for you yesterday evening Daddy."

No one said anything. Daddy was smiling questioningly at Ben but Ben just beamed innocently at Daddy; what else was there to say? I know a grin was spreading across my face. "Good old Ben," I was thinking, "say it like it is." Mum looked at the three of us, I didn't know what she was thinking. She quickly moved things along.

"Well, Miss Abigail," she said, smiling warmly at me, "and what do you have to say about your adventure?"

I hesitated. I really did not know how to put everything that had happened over these last few days into words. I was well aware that much had happened, that actually my life had completely changed. I didn't want to be dramatic but simply a re-telling of the events might miss the point.

Mum and Daddy looked at me, waiting. Ben was getting fidgety.

"Oh come on, Abi, get on with it. Where did you go last night?" Ben asked.

I laughed. "But it doesn't start with last night."

"Where does it start, Abi?" Daddy was looking at me very thoughtfully.

"I don't know. Maybe when I first saw Nic."

And so I told them about watching Nic running along the beach with Batman, free. Of meeting him, being scared of Batman. Of the light that shines even in the deepest darkness. The moon and the stars. Paddling in the sea, going to the rainforest, the bear, praying for Daddy, and my visit last night to the rainforest. In the end I did simply describe the events, but I couldn't seem to fully explain the effect they had on me. I was a bit shy about talking about God. We had never done that in my family. God had never figured in anything and had simply not ever been talked about.

"I can't explain it more than that at the moment," I finished. But I felt disappointed, that I'd tried to explain it all too soon. I knew I hadn't really expressed it properly.

We sat there. It felt awkward. Ben broke the silence.

"Did you really see a bear, Abi?" his eyes were wide. I nodded.

"You make a little visit to the edge of the wilderness and get to see a bear," said Daddy. "I spend days right in there and don't see sight nor sound of one. That is not fair," he pushed me playfully.

"That's because you made too much noise," I replied.

"So you know all about it now then," he said teasing.

When I looked at my mother I saw that there were tears in her eyes. Maybe I had explained it better than I thought.

nineteen

Of course for my family the evidence of my transformation was in front of their eyes day and night. I may not have explained what had happened very well, but that something had happened, and that it was tied up with this place and with Nic, was obvious. I'm not sure I realised how obvious at first. I mean I knew I was changed, no one knew better than me that I was beginning to live for the first time in my life. But because so much else had been going on with Daddy missing and coming back, I simply don't think I realised how obvious it was to everyone else. It had been a process, a fast process, but a process, and it's hard to see that through other people's eyes when it's your experience, your process.

For Mum the change was welcome and a great relief but also hard to deal with. It was a huge change for her. My ability to cope with things had always had to be a top consideration when anything was going to be done, or when we were going out anywhere. Ben would always fit in, but I always had to be fitted around. No more nights of getting up to me, maybe several times a night. She no longer had to be on edge, worrying that something might easily upset me. But there was something else as well.

After breakfast the next morning Ben and Daddy were out on the beach playing chase as noisily as possible. I was helping Mum clear up the breakfast things. We could hear Ben squealing loudly and we both looked up and laughed. We stood and watched them for a while. Mum put her arm round my shoulders and held me to her as we watched. Finally she said, "Do you know what I find really hard to get my head round, Abi?" I looked at her. She carried on, "that you're not dependent on me any more. I don't mean I want you to be. But . . ." she paused. "It's difficult to know how to put it. I feel almost redundant."

"But, Mum," I began to say.

"No," she interrupted shaking her head vigorously. "It's not you, darling. It's just that you've needed me in a special way for so long. Now I need to find a new role as mother of a maturing ten-year-old daughter. I don't expect you to understand, Abi. Does this make any sense?"

I thought about it for a while. I began to see it, as well as I could, from my mum's point of view. I nodded my head and hugged her. "Is it like the world around you is changing and you haven't quite caught up with it?"

She laughed, really laughed, a care-free laugh. "Yes," she said, "that's what it's like."

Daddy, on the other hand, had no misgivings at all. He was delighted, he could begin to do with me all the things he had longed to do. I took him to the boardwalk in the rainforest – just me and him. Even though he had been into the depths of the rainforest by himself, it was special to take him. We ran down to the sea and he gently splashed me at the water's edge. Then he picked me up and pretended he was going to throw me into the sea. I screamed, but it was an OK kind of a scream – I was laughing as well. And he, himself, had changed. He seemed more light-hearted and more confident, I think, although it was hard to pin-point exactly.

Ben, too, was delighted at having a sister who was a bit more fun. "Abi," he said to me thoughtfully. "I loved you before but I love you differently now."

"What do you mean?" I asked.

"Well," he replied trying to find the words. "You're more you." I think I understood.

Ben and I wore Daddy out on the beach that day. Playing all kinds of games and paddling in the sea. When he came to kiss me goodnight he sat on the edge of my bed and looked at me for a long while. Neither of us said anything. Eventually he smiled and said quietly, "I have a new daughter."

"Am I a new daughter, Daddy?" I asked him wondering. "I feel so different but I still feel like me. Do you understand?"

"I think so," he said. "Maybe it's not so much that you're a new daughter or a new you, but more the person you were always meant to be. Somehow the real you got trapped in the fears."

"Yes," I said. I thought about it. "Yes, that's what it feels like."

"Abi?" he said in a completely different tone of voice.

"Yes," I answered, wondering what was coming.

"I'd like to take you and Ben whale-watching tomorrow."

"Whale-watching?" I asked laughing. "How do you do that?"

"Well, you get taken out in a boat. And these people kind of know where the whales are and you can watch them. It's supposed to be really good. What do you think?"

I hesitated. "Is it a big boat?" I asked.

"Well, that depends, Abi," he replied. He began to get excited. "You can go on zodiacs that seat eight or ten or twelve people. They're fun, they go really fast and hit against the waves." He saw my face and stopped. "Oh," he said, then laughed. "It's OK, Abi, they have big, slow boats, too, that hold about fifty people." He smiled and took my hand. "Sweetheart, it's really safe. They wouldn't take tourists out in them otherwise. Hey, Ben would be too small for a zodiac anyway."

"He'd love it though," I said.

Dad nodded. "He would. But those bigger boats have rails all the way round. And they don't smack into the waves."

"Do the whales come close, Daddy?" I asked, still unsure.

He spoke carefully, I knew he would always be honest with me. "I guess. But it's a sturdy boat. They wouldn't tip the boat over or anything. And the deck is a long way up. You'd get a good view but you wouldn't be too near them."

"I can't swim, Dad."

"I'll be there. I will take care of you." He still had hold of my hand, he squeezed it. "We'll all have life jackets. There are lots of other boats out there at the same time."

For the first time since I had come back from my night trip to the rainforest with Nic I had a sense of panic. I wasn't going to scream or anything, but I could feel fear creeping around my stomach. I worried that I had not truly conquered my fear and that I would spoil it for Daddy and be afraid. "Daddy," I said, "would you mind if I let you know in the morning? A boat on the sea's a big thing."

"Bigger than being faced with a bear or the rainforest at night?"

"I don't know," was all I could say.

"That's fine, Abi. You tell me in the morning. Goodnight, sleep well." And he kissed my forehead.

I lay awake awhile that night. Thinking about going out on the sea in a boat. I had conquered my fear of the sea in some ways. I was happy to paddle in it and stand at the edge looking at the great expanse. But to go on a boat. The vastness of the sea struck me as so overwhelming. Could I do it? Then it was as if I could hear Nic's voice: "There is always a light even in the deepest darkness." Fragments of things Nic had said that night in the rainforest went round in my head. "You have lived all your life in darkness . . . The darkness is vast . . . Darkness is everywhere all around. No matter how hard you try, you can't make it small enough to live with . . . You can't change the darkness but you can carry light, and where that light is there isn't any darkness." I remembered that God had

epilogue

It is eight years since that first family visit to Vancouver Island. This is the first time I've been back since. We've never been back as a family – I think, for my parents, the first time we came was such an important time, that they have wanted to keep it as a special memory.

As soon as I started thinking about taking a year off between school and university, I knew what I wanted to do – to come back here and do conservation work in the rainforest.

On my first evening here, I stood on the beach where I first put my feet in the sea and thought about Nic and Batman and all that happened during that amazing summer. If it hadn't been for coming here and meeting Nic and him showing me so much about myself and about God, I would never be going to university at all. And I wouldn't be doing a gap year.

When I remember how fearful I was of everything, it's amazing that I'm going to university. It would have been impossible, if I hadn't changed. I'm nervous about it, but not scared. Now I know that I'm not really ever by myself and even when things seem dark, there is always a light that shines. I'm excited.

I haven't seen Nic again since I've been back. And I haven't been able to find out anything about him. As a child, details of surnames and addresses never came up. I continued to see much of Nic during the rest of our stay on Vancouver Island. He taught me so well to love this place and the wildness. He also taught me well to love his God. I have such a special place in my heart for Nic. He accepted me as I was but was bold enough to face me with the truth of myself. And he knew the way out of the darkness.

Also available from Dernier Publishing:

I Want to be an Airline Pilot
by Mary Weeks Millard

Shema, an eight-year-old Rwandan goatherd from a child-led family, has many adventures, including a goat eating his only T-shirt, a frightening visit to a medicine man and a dangerously close brush with a spitting black cobra! Through them all, little by little, Shema learns about "Mister God" and discovers that although he is an orphan, he has a Father in heaven who cares for him. A victorious, heart-warming story for 8–11s, with lovely background to life in rural Rwanda.

"I give this book 10/10" – Ellen

"A thrilling adventure story about three orphans' dreams coming true when their prayers were answered." – Jonathan

"I think this book is very good, it made me feel happy, sad and really excited; I think the most interesting part is when Shema killed the black cobra. It was also very moving when in the book Ishimwe starts to cry because her parents died. I really enjoyed this book, it is one of my favourites." – Kemi

ISBN 978 0 9536963 5 2

Available from your local book shop or on-line
www.dernierpublishing.com

Beech Bank Girls – Every Girl Has A Story by Eleanor Watkins

Six teenage friends draw nearer to God and to each other in these fun, moving and honest accounts. Annie, Willow, Rachel, Holly, Amber and Chloe share their laughter, their tears, their hopes, their fears and their secrets with each other and with us. Miracle and party included! Christian chick lit for ages 10–14

> "*Beech Bank Girls* is a very interesting book, dealing with a whole number of situations encountered by teenage girls. It portrays well the struggles that girls have and at the same time helps to show what to do in each situation. I would recommend this book as I really enjoyed it and found it helpful at the same time." – Claire

> "I loved reading about the different girls' lives and how they struggled with different problems at school, at home and with their Christian lives. It also teaches more about God, like how he knows each and every one of us, he loves us all, listens to us and will help us with everything." – Emma

ISBN 978 0 9536963 4 5

London's Gone
by J. M. Evans

London has been bombed by terrorists. Maria watched in horror as the smoke rose from the direction of London. Now she must make a hazardous journey to safety with her sister and a Christian friend, but is anywhere safe now? For Maria, the journey is also inside herself as she begins to discover a side to life that she did not know existed. A thrilling drama full of suspense. For ages 12+

"I just couldn't put this book down!" – Jilly

"I found the story very tense and compelling." – Sandy

"A roller coaster ride of adventure that I found difficult to put down. The characters were well developed and it was great to see how their relationships with each other changed and grew as the story went on. A great read and a book I would thoroughly recommend." – Jo

"Scary, because it could actually happen." – Laura

ISBN 978 0 9536963 2 1

The Treasure Hunt
by J. M. Evans

Ravi, Debbie, Joel and Lance's first exciting mystery adventure. Who is in the back of the white lorry and why are they there? Prayer, faith and their Bible knowledge all help, but when the case takes an unexpected turn, the friends also need to be courageous and obedient. Will they find out what is going on and find the real treasure? For ages 8–11

"The best book I've ever read!" – Emily

"Brilliant!" – Ben

"A truly inspiring Christian story." – Hannah

"This is a really good story. I couldn't stop reading it. I liked the mystery and it was full of suspense. Some of the characters were quite funny at times." – Lydia

ISBN 978 0 9536963 1 4

Mystery in the Snow
by J. M. Evans

Not long after solving their first mystery (*The Treasure Hunt*), Ravi, Debbie, Lance and Joel find themselves with another problem; Ravi's shed has been burgled. Can they find out who did it? The plot thickens as an old lady's handbag goes missing, then a cat disappears. Can all these things be connected? Join the Christian friends as they find answers in unexpected places. For ages 8–11

> "So exciting that I couldn't put it down!" – Lydia

> "There are some books that can be boring, but this book made me want to carry on reading. I would definitely recommend it." – Joshua

> "I really enjoyed reading *Mystery in the Snow* because I like mystery and Christian books and found this one very exciting, adventurous and mysterious. I like how it teaches that when people pray and obey God they can make a difference in other people's lives. I think it is good having the same characters as the first book and how they always pray for help in what they should do. This story would appeal to people who like adventure and mystery books." – Emma

ISBN 978 0 9536963 3 8